At the Park

First published in 2010
by Wayland

Text copyright © Annemarie Young
Illustration copyright © Louise Redshaw

Wayland
338 Euston Road
London NW1 3BH

Wayland Australia
Level 17/207 Kent Street
Sydney, NSW 2000

Series Editor: Louise John
Editor: Katie Powell
Cover design: Paul Cherrill
Design: D.R.ink
Consultant: Shirley Bickler

A CIP catalogue record for this book is available from the British Library.

ISBN 9780750260398

Printed in China

Wayland is a division of Hachette Children's Books,
an Hachette UK Company

www.hachette.co.uk

At the Park

Written by Annemarie Young
Illustrated by Louise Redshaw

WAYLAND

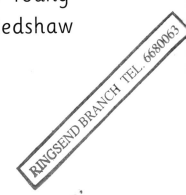

We saw a brown duck
at the park.

We saw a white dog
at the park.

We saw a black bird
at the park.

We saw a red kite
at the park.

We saw a yellow hat
at the park.

We saw a blue butterfly
at the park.

We saw a pink flower
at the park.

We saw a green leaf
at the park.

We saw a green
caterpillar on the leaf!

21

Guiding a First Read of
At the Park

It is important to talk through the book with the child before they read it alone. This prepares them for the way the story unfolds, and allows them to enjoy the pictures as you both talk naturally, using the language they will later encounter when reading. Read the brief overview below, and then follow the suggestions:

1. Talking through the book
The family went for a walk and they saw lots of different coloured things at the park.

Let's read the title: **At the Park**
Now turn to page 4. Here is the family.
What could they see on the water?
The family said, "We saw a brown
duck at the park."
Let's look at the next page.
What did the family see here?
Yes, it's a white dog. What do you think they said? Yes, "We saw a white dog at the park."

Continue through the book, guiding the discussion to fit the text as the child looks at the illustrations.

On page 18, the family said, "We saw a green leaf at the park." And on the last page, what was on the leaf? Yes, a green caterpillar!

2. A first reading of the book

Ask the child to read the book independently, pointing carefully under each word (tracking), while thinking about the story. Praise attempts by the child to correct themselves, and prompt them to use their letter knowledge, the punctuation and check the meaning, for example:

Did your pointing fit the words you said?
Go back and try again.

You said, "in the park". Yes, that makes sense.
Now try again and look a bit more carefully.

If necessary, tell the child the word 'at' and then
ask them to check and reread the sentence.

3. Follow-up activities

The high frequency words in this title are:
a   at   saw   the   we

- Select a new high frequency word, and ask the child or group to find it throughout the book. Discuss the shape of the letters and the letter sounds.
- To memorise the word, ask the child to write it in the air, then write it repeatedly on a whiteboard or on paper, leaving a space between each attempt.

4. Encourage

- Reading the book again – with expression.
- Drawing a picture based on the story.
- Writing one or two sentences using the practised word.

START READING is a series of highly enjoyable books for beginner readers. **The books have been carefully graded to match the Book Bands widely used in schools.** This enables readers to be sure they choose books that match their own reading ability.

Look out for the Band colour on the book in our Start Reading logo.

The Bands are:

Pink Band 1A & 1B

Red Band 2

Yellow Band 3

Blue Band 4

Green Band 5

Orange Band 6

Turquoise Band 7

Purple Band 8

Gold Band 9

START READING books can be read independently or shared with an adult. They promote the enjoyment of reading through satisfying stories supported by fun illustrations.

Annemarie Young lives in Cambridge but grew up in a city by the sea. She and her family like going for walks whatever the weather, building sand castles and finding all sorts of bugs in the garden.

Louise Redshaw likes to go for long walks and eat picnic lunches with friends when she's not too busy drawing. She loves animals but likes donkeys the most and one day wants to have a huge garden where she can keep her own donkey.